Dedicated to the Centenary Children's Ministry

Dapple Grey Books
1006 Royal Crest Dr.
Richmond, Kentucky 40475

Library of Congress Control Number: 2017937037
Relich, Christina
Herman to the Rescue/Written and Illustrated by Christina Relich
Summary: A little fish named Herman helps a baby whale back home,
discovering that he can do great things regardless of size.
ISBN 978-0-9987722-0-2

First Printing: 2017
Printed in the United States of America

Herman to the Rescue!

By Christina Relich

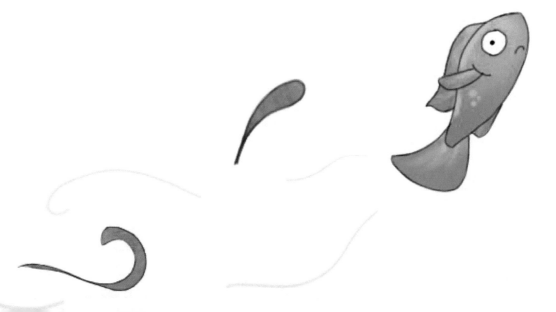

Herman was a fish.
A very small fish in a very big ocean.

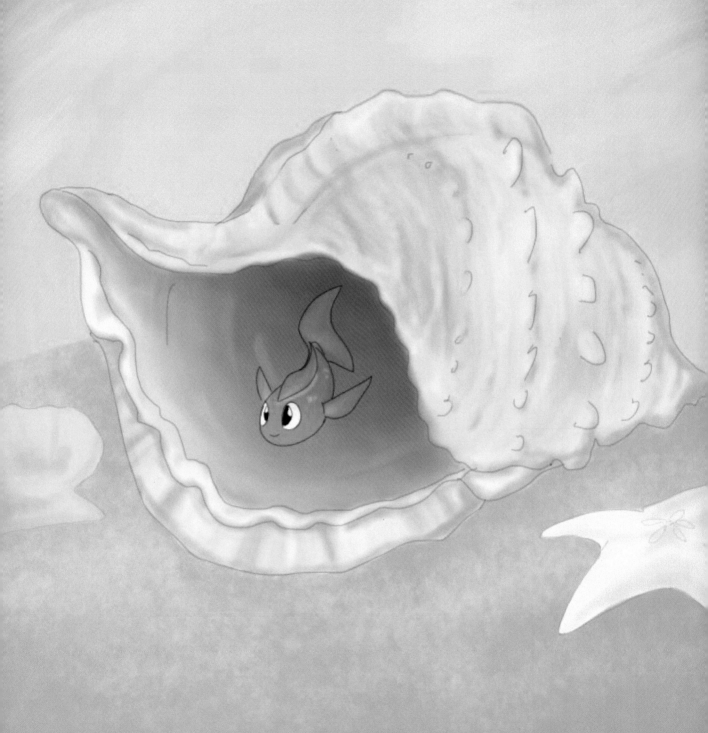

Every morning, Herman would go visit his friend, Mr. Tang. Mr. Tang always had something nice to say to little Herman, and today was no different.

"Remember this verse, Herman!" said Mr. Tang at the end of their visit. "The Lord on high is mightier than the waves of the sea!"

Herman swam back to his house to think.

"If God is so big and strong," he wondered, "why would He worry about someone as little as me? Wouldn't He care more about big fish and whales?"

This made Herman sad.

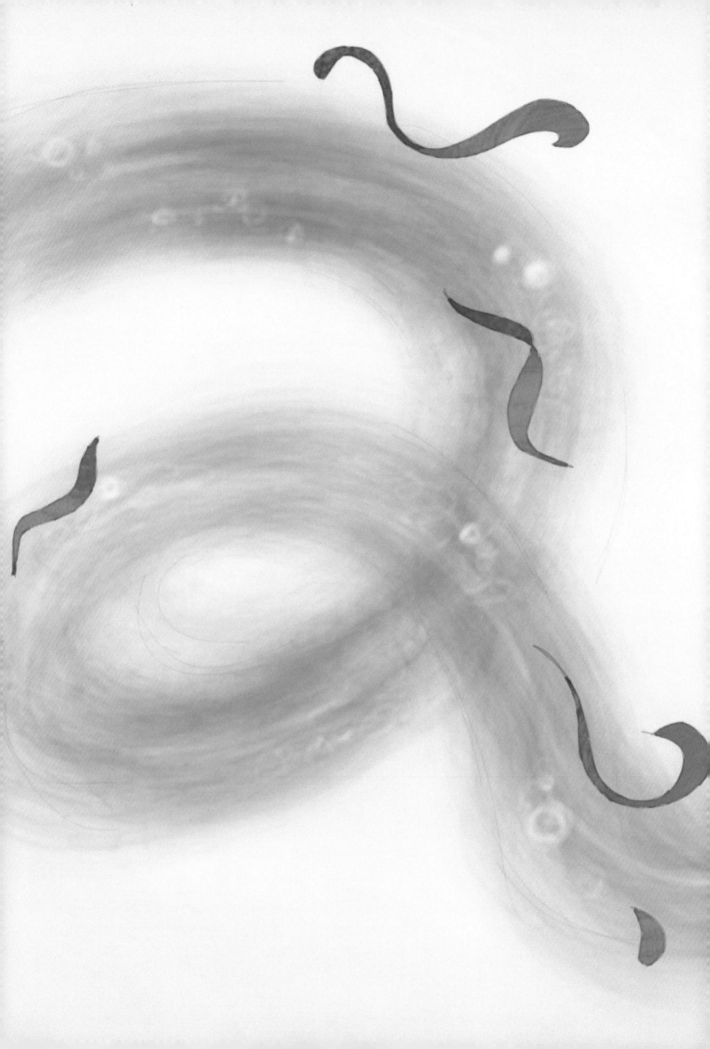

But, Herman was thinking so hard that he didn't even see the Big Current, and swam right in!

The fast water swept him far away...

Past Lenny Lionfish...

Past Mr. and Mrs.
Seahorse…

Through a big coral hole...

And right onto a turtle's back!

"Woah," said Herman, feeling dizzy.

The big turtle turned his head. "Eh? Oh, hi there, little fish! Looks like the Big Current's causing trouble again!"

"What?" Herman asked. "Someone else got swept away?"

"Why yes, see over there?" said the turtle, pointing with his fin.

Behind a big rock, a little baby whale was crying.

"Oh, where oh where am I?" she sniffed. "I wanna go home!"

Herman was a little afraid to talk to the whale, who was much bigger than he was. But, Herman didn't want to see anyone so sad. He slowly swam up to her.

"H-hi. Excuse me? Miss whale?" said Herman softly.

The little orca looked up. "Oh!" she said. "A tiny fish!"

"My name's Herman" said Herman. "And...I am tiny...but I've seen where the big whales like to swim. It's right by my house, and your mommy and daddy might be there. I could show you!"

"Oh, YES! Oh yes oh yes!" shouted the whale, smiling brightly as she twirled in the water. "I'd love you to show me! My name's Macy by the way."

"N-nice to meet you, Macy," said Herman, a little dizzy from Macy's spinning. "Now, follow me! Let's see if I remember the way..."

And so, they said
goodbye to Mr. Turtle...

Swam through the
big coral hole...

Past the
Seahorse couple...

And right into
Macy's parents!

Past Lenny Lionfish...

"Mommy! Daddy! My new friend got me back home!" said Macy, twirling around again.

"Oh, thank the Lord for this little fish!" said Macy's Mommy. "We're very blessed!"

Herman was confused. "But, I'm so small. Am I really that important?"

"Of course you are!" said Macy's Daddy. "You're not too small for us, and you're definitely not too small for God!"

"And by His strength," said Macy's Mommy, "He guided you both home!"

A little later, Herman swam back home.

He'd been through the Big Current, made a new friend, and helped her back home, all in one day!

There's no way I did that all by myself, thought Herman, looking at the bright lights of the sea. *The whales were right. God is looking out for me after all!*

Herman remembered the verse Mr. Tang taught him: "The Lord on high is mightier than the waves of the sea."

And Herman didn't feel so small anymore.

CPSIA information can be obtained at www.ICGtesting.com
Printed in the USA
LVIW01n0254240317
528337LV00006B/13